W9-BLO-005

The Lighthouse Children

Story and Pictures by Syd Hoff

HarperTrophy®
A Division of HarperCollins*Publishers*

HarperCollins®, 🐎®, Harper Trophy®, and I Can Read Book®
are trademarks of HarperCollins Publishers Inc.

The Lighthouse Children
Copyright © 1994 by Syd Hoff
Printed in the U.S.A. All rights reserved.
Library of Congress Cataloging-in-Publication Data
Hoff, Syd, date.
The lighthouse children / story and pictures by Syd Hoff.
      p.   cm. — (An I can read book)
   Summary: When an old lighthouse keeper and his wife leave their
seaside home, they find a way for their old friends, the seagulls,
to find them.
   ISBN 0-06-022958-6. — ISBN 0-06-022959-4 (lib. bdg.)
   ISBN 0-06-444178-4 (pbk.)
   1. Lighthouse keepers—Fiction.   2. Gulls—Fiction.]   I. Title.
II. Series.
PZ7.H672Lf   1994   94-41172
[E]—dc20   CIP
                                                                         AC
Typography by Al Cetta
❖
First Harper Trophy edition, 1996.

For D.B.H.,

the gull of my dreams

By the edge of the sea,

a lighthouse stood all alone.

An old couple lived there.

They were named Sam and Rose.

At night they shone a beam of light

to guide the ships that passed.

Sam and Rose

did not have any children,

but they were never lonely.

They had sea gulls.

A hundred sea gulls flew in every day
to look for food and a place to land.

"Eat this, Ernie and Bernie,"

said Sam.

"It's good for you, Dora and Cora,"

said Rose.

They made sure that the sea gulls

never went hungry.

"Be careful on those rocks,

Hank, Frank, Molly, and Dolly!"

called Sam.

"Watch it in the water,

Lanny, Nanny, Helga, and Zelga!"

called Rose.

The sea gulls loved the old couple
and were glad to pose for them.

But sea gulls can't stay in one place
very long.

Soon they spread their wings
and flew away.

"Don't worry, Rose," said Sam.

"Our sea gulls will come back."

"I know," said Rose.

"We will see them tomorrow."

12

They shone a beam of light

across the water.

They sounded their foghorn.

They made sure that it was safe

for ships to pass at night.

13

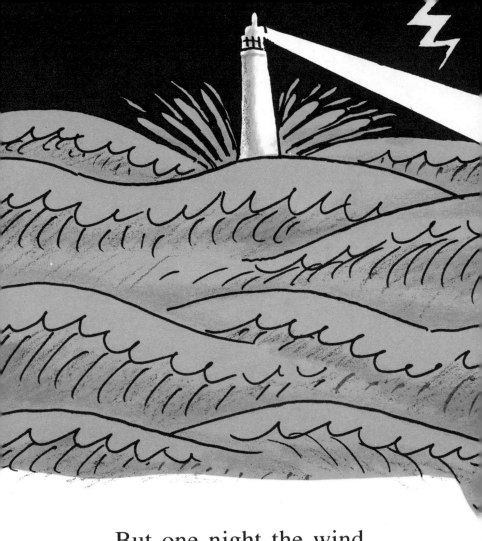

But one night the wind

started to blow.

Giant waves crashed down

on the lighthouse.

14

The storm went on and on.

In the morning,

Sam and Rose looked over the damage.

There were holes in the walls

and the roof was almost gone.

"We can't fix all this,"

said Sam.

"I guess it's time for us

to move on," said Rose.

17

They packed their things

and moved away.

They found a plain house
far from the edge of the sea.

There were green hills all around

and tall trees

and neighbors who came to visit.

20

There were parties and cookouts.

The old couple was never lonely,

but they missed their sea gulls.

21

"We need our birds,"
said Sam.

"I wish they would come visit,
but they are so far away.
How will they ever find us?"

"I know what we can do,"
said Rose.

"We can tell our birds
where we are!"

So the old couple shone

a beam of light from their house.

Then they waited and waited.

One day the sound of birds was heard
in the sky.

Everybody ran to look.

"Bill, Jill, Bonnie, Connie,

Ann, and Fran!

We are so glad you found us!"

said Sam.

"Did you miss us, Jack, Mack,

Lenny, Henny, Luke, and Duke?"

asked Rose.

They fed their sea gulls.

The neighbors fed them too.

But sea gulls can't stay in one place
very long.

Soon they spread their wings
and flew away.

"Will the sea gulls come back?"
asked the neighbors.

"Of course they will come back!"

said Sam.

"They are our lighthouse children,"

said Rose.

And the old couple
kept the light shining
from their house,
just to make sure.